THE LEGEND OF LEFI GANDERSON

THE GOAT BOY OF MOUNT SEETHING

Dedicated to Amelie 'Millie' Lewis,

& to Ann (MLW) & Tim

& the Homage de Fromage Cheese Club

Thank you to the residents, young & old of Seething,

Written by Robin Hutchinson

Illustrated by Rosalind Maroney

Additional ideas by Paul Day and other residents of Seething in Surbiton

Published by Homage Publishing
Text © Robin Hutchinson
Illustration © Rosalind Maroney

If a bird were to have
flown over Mount Seething it
would have looked down upon a
beautiful land of green fields, tall trees
and a sparkling river.
But a bird would never dare to fly over Mount Seething because living at the very top was a Gian
A Giant whose heart was as dark as his hair and the Giant's name was Thamas Deeton.

Thamas was rarely at home because giants spend most of their time staying with their relatives. But every four years he would return to his home at the top of Mount Seething and terrorise the villagers who lived at the foot of the mountain. He would destroy their crops and frighten their animals and when that was done he would go away again, leaving the village to recover and to wait for his return.

One day when
Thamas left to visit his Uncle, the
Giant of St Michael's Mount, something
strange happened. The Villagers heard crying from a
cave at the bottom of the mountain. When they went near
they saw a tiny baby wrapped in a blanket on the ground. The
women rushed forward to comfort the baby but when they did the
blanket fell open and they saw a terrible sight. For in their hands they
held a small goat boy with horns upon his head and coarse golden
hair growing down his back.

The grown ups in the village shrank back from the little child
because the giant had made them fearful of strangers.
"We must leave - whatever this is - in the cave.
It is nothing to do with us,"
they said and they went back to rebuild their village
and tried to forget the little goat boy.

When the adults had gone the children went
back and the little goat boy smiled at them
and won their hearts.

The children loved the little goat boy. Every day they took him food and drink and very quickly the little goat boy grew as strong and tall as them. The children took him all the scraps that were thrown away by the grown ups and he made the most beautiful clothes and toys from them. The children decided to call the little goat boy 'Lefti' because he used his left hand to make these wonderful things.

ut of all the things the little goat boy did, one seemed like magic to the children. When they brought him milk to drink he would do the strangest thing. He would take the milk and warm and cool it and pass it from wooden bowl to wooden bowl. Before long it would become both a solid and a liquid. From the solid he could make a hard yellow food that tasted more wonderful than anything the children had tasted before.

One day the river of Seething turned black and a terrible smell came from the 'land of the berries' and the children knew at once that the giant Thamas Deeton was washing his dirty smelly feet in the river and would soon return. The children told Lefti all about the giant and tried to make him hide but he would not. As the giant's footsteps got nearer the children ran away but Lefti just stood and looked up at the enormous Thamas Deeton.

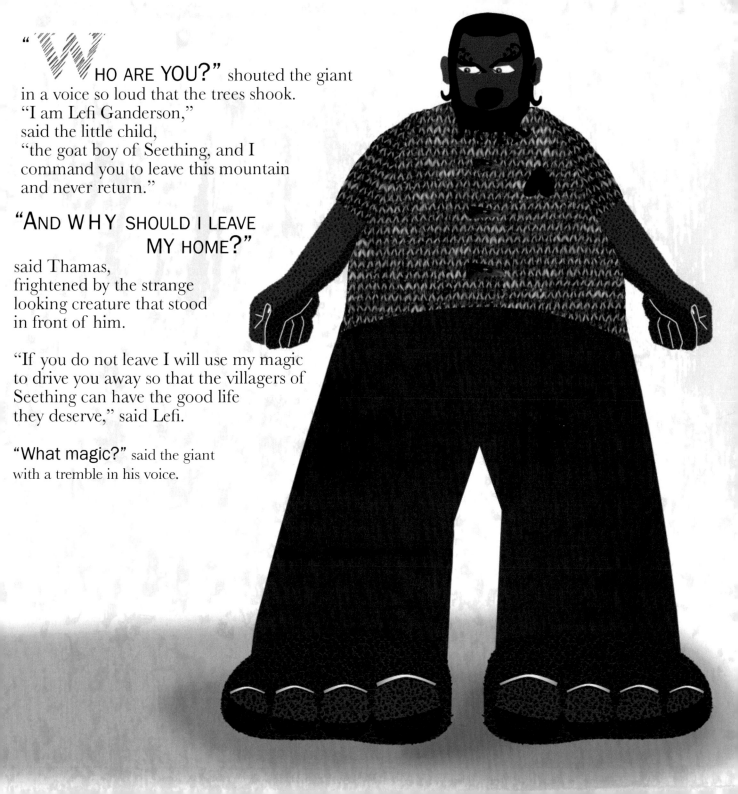

"**W**HO ARE YOU?**" shouted the giant
in a voice so loud that the trees shook.
"I am Lefi Ganderson,"
said the little child,
"the goat boy of Seething, and I
command you to leave this mountain
and never return."

"**AND WHY SHOULD I LEAVE
MY HOME?**"

said Thamas,
frightened by the strange
looking creature that stood
in front of him.

"If you do not leave I will use my magic
to drive you away so that the villagers of
Seething can have the good life
they deserve," said Lefi.

"**What magic?**" said the giant
with a tremble in his voice.

" I will do nothing to harm you yet," said Lefi, "but I shall show you my power." With that Lefi took a tiny golden ring that shone bright in the sun off his finger and held it up to Thamas. "If I can live for one year from the food that can pass through the middle of this tiny ring then you must leave." The giant stared at the tiny golden ring and at Lefi. He thought about all the meat and bread and vegetables that he would need to eat and stared at the ring. He knew that nobody could live **even for a week on** the food that could pass through the tiny hole.

"I accept your challenge," said Thamas "for no one but a magician could live on so little food. I think you will die trying and the Mountain will be mine once again and then I will make life even worse for the villagers as a punishment for sheltering you."

With that the people from the village who had gathered to hear the shouting looked at each other and began to tremble. "We did not help the Goat Boy!" they shouted. Lefi looked at them and smiled, "But I shall help you. Bring me all the milk you have." he said to the children.

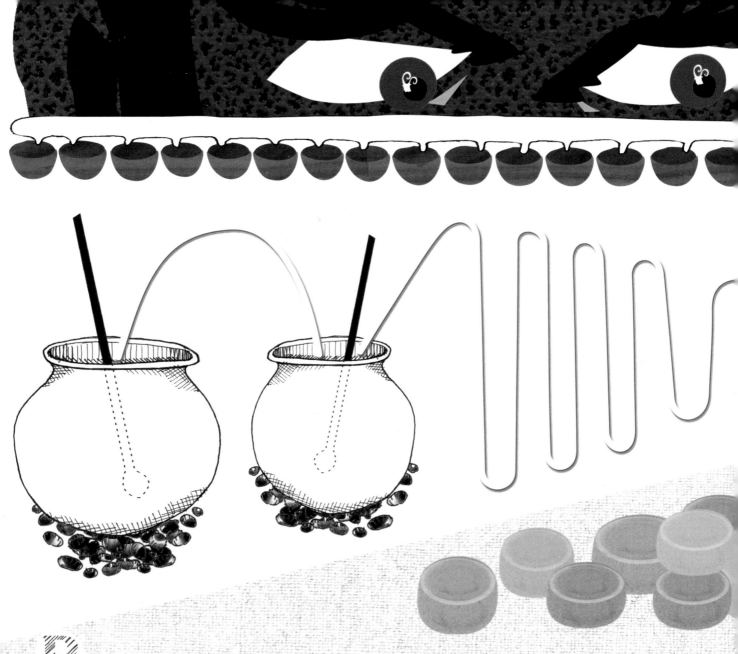

By the time the children came back with the milk Lefi had placed twenty-nine wooden bowls on the ground. He held the tiny golden ring between his thumb and his finger and with a little white jug began to pour the milk through the middle of the golden hoop into the bowls. The giant began to think that he might have been tricked.

"Sit down," said Lefi, "this will take some time, because the real magic happens now."

hamas and all the villagers watched as Lefi warmed and cooled the milk and poured it from bowl to bowl until they saw it begin to separate into curds and whey. Lefi took the solid creamy mass and began to push it together. As he did he chuckled, then the chuckle became a laugh and then he laughed and laughed until he had made twenty-nine round shapes of the solid yellow mass. Lefi took a tiny piece and put it in his mouth. "That will be enough food for me today," he said "and these twenty nine would feed you and me for a year".

Thamas Deeton stood up to his full height and stamped on the ground. The villagers were terrified but Lefi knew that a giant can never break his word.

"You have TRICKED me goat boy," said Thamas, "but my word is my bond. I shall leave Seething but not before I HAVE SMASHED DOWN MY MOUNTAIN."

With that Thamas lifted his mighty fists and began to beat at Mount Seething. Rocks and boulders began to fly miles into the air and soon all that was left was little Lefi's cave.

The giant brought
down his mighty fist and
nothing was left of Lefi's home.

Thamas Deeton turned and stormed away,
making the ground shake with his anger.

He was so cross that he did not see the rock from Lefi's cave flying through the air.
Just as Thamas was crossing the river the rock fell from the sky hitting the giant on the head
and his body fell dead into the river.
It was so big that it made a new island for the water to flow round – Thamas Deeton Isle.

The villagers came out of their hiding places and cheered but as they turned to thank Lefi they realised that he was not there. Where his cave had once stood was just a hollow in the ground and there lying at the bottom was Lefi's little golden ring. The villagers were very sad. They realised that they had treated the little goat boy very badly. They had not welcomed him, they had not shared their food or their homes or anything. They had even been horrible to him as he was saving them from the giant.

The Leader of the village spoke. "Villagers of Seething,' she said, "We must learn from today and never behave like this again. Seething must become a village that is open to all. It should not matter what you look like, where you come from or who you are – you will be welcome here and Lefi has shown us the way."
With that she picked up the tiny ring from the ground and from where it had lain a small spring of water began to rise. "This ring is a symbol of love. We shall not forget what Lefi did. We shall hold a festival every year to celebrate him driving the giant away."

And so the very first Seething Festival was held that very day. The children showed the adults how to eat the yellow food that Lefi called 'cheese'. They taught the grown ups the songs that Lefi had taught them. They laughed and danced and sang songs around a big bonfire. That evening they decided that they should make 'cheese' as Lefi had shown them and that they would chuckle as Lefi had because their life was now so much better.

The villagers decided that once, every four years, there would be an extra
special day in the year to remember when Lefi defeated the giant. That day would be called
after what Lefi had said in front of the giant - the 'Twenty-Nine Fed You and Me'.
On this extra special day they decided that all the villagers must do something to help someone
else and do it with a happy heart knowing that true love is doing good things for others.
"Our hearts shall leap with happiness when we help others," said the villagers.

So every year the Village of Seething held their festival. Every fourth year they had a special day to remind them to help others in their community.

Now some years later Lefi's golden ring went missing and soon after that, as people's lives became busier and more selfish, the villagers of Seething stopped holding the Festival and forgot all about Lefi.

But we will not forget and the signs are still there if you look on a map or visit the area or just think about some of the things that happen today.

irstly there is no mountain in Seething anymore.

Thamas Deeton Isle became Thames Ditton Island and land around named Thames Ditton.

The first cheese in the world was made by Lefi. A 'chuckle of cheese' is now called a truckle of cheese.

The area where the villagers made their cheese was called Cheesington and is now known as Chessington.

The "land of berries" became known as Berrylands and even today if the wind is in the right direction you can smell the terrible aroma of the ghost of Thamas Deeton returning.

The little spring of water from where Lefi's ring had lain gave the name Seething Wells to the area.

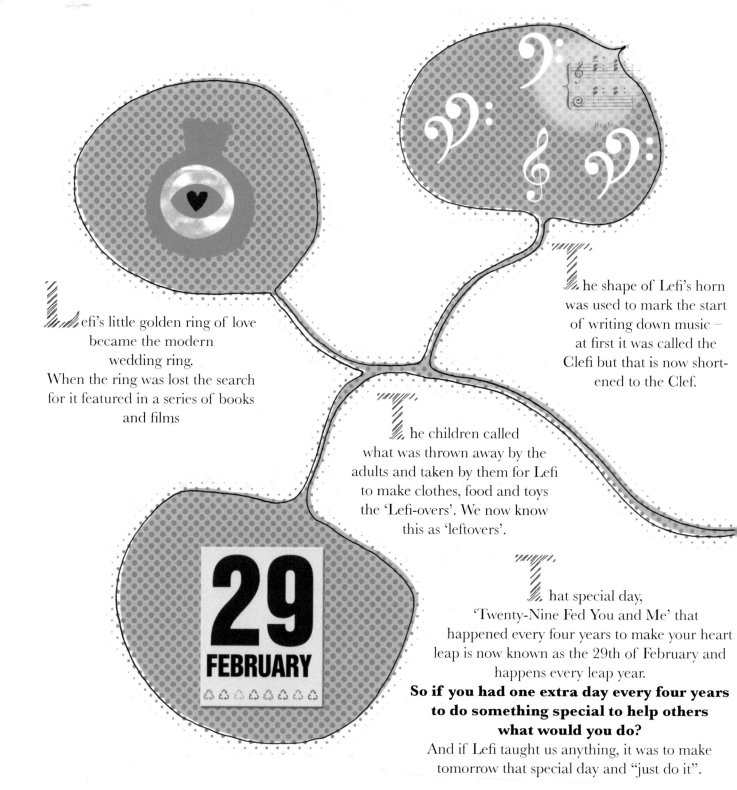

Lefi's little golden ring of love became the modern wedding ring.
When the ring was lost the search for it featured in a series of books and films

The shape of Lefi's horn was used to mark the start of writing down music – at first it was called the Clefi but that is now short-ened to the Clef.

The children called what was thrown away by the adults and taken by them for Lefi to make clothes, food and toys the 'Lefi-overs'. We now know this as 'leftovers'.

That special day, 'Twenty-Nine Fed You and Me' that happened every four years to make your heart leap is now known as the 29th of February and happens every leap year.

So if you had one extra day every four years to do something special to help others what would you do?

And if Lefi taught us anything, it was to make tomorrow that special day and "just do it".

29 FEBRUARY

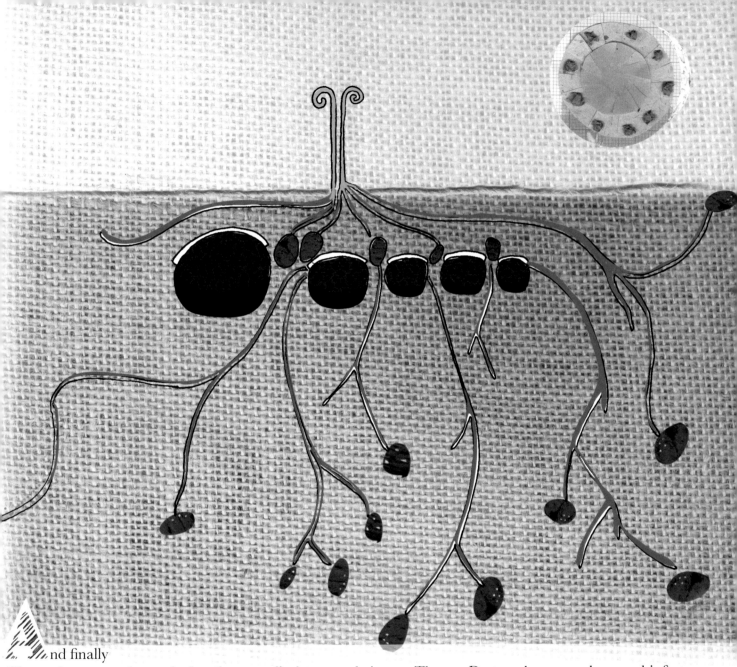

nd finally

Giants always row about who has the most dirt between their toes. Thamas Deeton always won because his feet were filthy from walking around the land. When Thamas died and his body became covered with soil a strange plant grew from between his toes. No one really knows where it came from but this plant produced oddly shaped fruit under the ground. This fruit was good to eat when roasted in a fire. If you sprinkled strong cheese on top some people said it smelt like the giant's toes. Yes, the first potatoes in the world grew in Seething from between the giant's toes and jacket potato and cheese is still a favourite Seething meal! And that is what is called a 'footnote'.

Is there a place in your heart for Lefi?

Thank you Christina Gardner and Dave "Don't eat those grapes - they haven't been washed" Springle
and everyone who made the Seething Festival of 2010 possible